For my fruitcake friends,
Kate and Karen
C.D.S.

For Matt, Dan & Lewis,
my favorite people
D.G.K.

Text copyright © 2002 by Carol Diggory Shields
Illustrations copyright © 2002 by Doreen Gay-Kassel
All rights reserved
CIP Data is available

All trademark names in this text
are the property of their respective owners.

Published in the United States in 2002
by Handprint Books
413 Sixth Avenue
Brooklyn, New York 11215
www.handprintbooks.com

Design and digital manipulation by Ellen M. Lucaire

First Edition
Printed in China
ISBN: 1-929766-29-7
4 6 8 10 9 7 5 3

FOOD FIGHT!

BY CAROL DIGGORY SHIELDS

ILLUSTRATED BY DOREEN GAY-KASSEL

HANDPRINT BOOKS BROOKLYN, NEW YORK

Last night when
you were fast asleep,
snoring unawares,

Do you know
what happened
in the kitchen
downstairs?

Just about midnight
or a little bit later
The light came on
in your refrigerator.

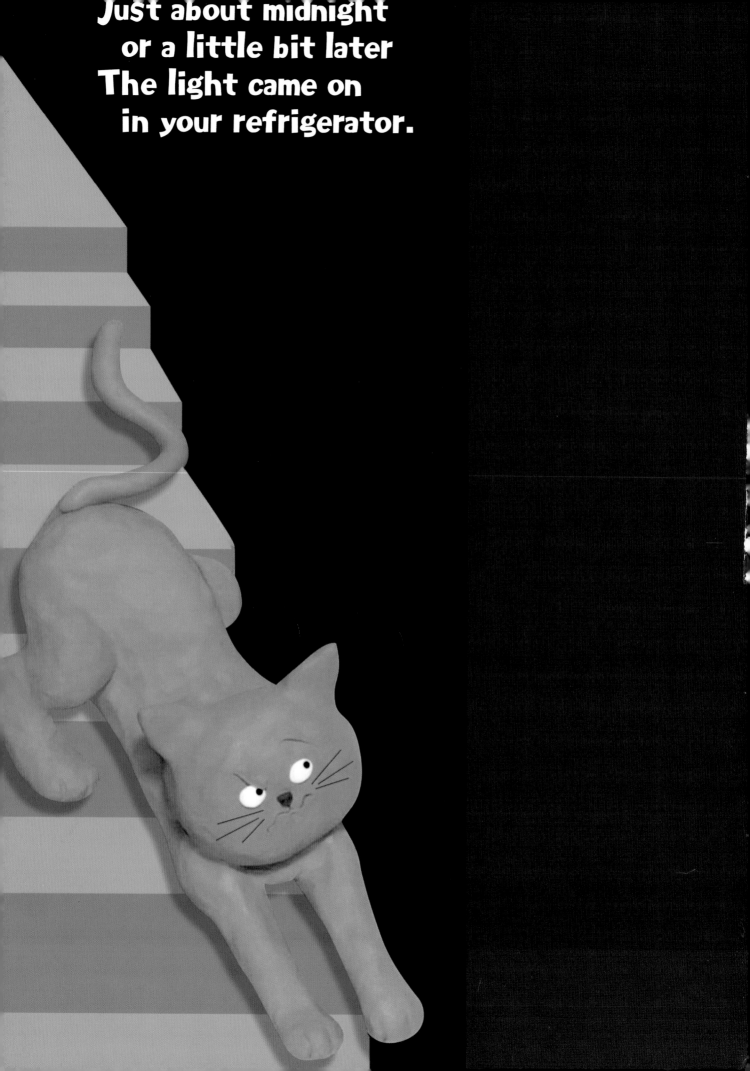

The milk peeked out and whispered,

"ALL CLEAR!"

"CLOSE THE DOOR!"

yelled the ranch,

"I'M DRESSING IN HERE!"

"THIS PLACE IS THE PITS!"

all the olives cried, Celery stalked to the door, and opened it wide.

"LETTUCE HAVE A PARTY!"

And slid to the floor said the Salad greens, on a bunch of string beans.

The **coffee** perked up and the **beets** started thumping,

The **bread** made a toast and the **jello** was jumping.

The almonds acted nutty, the pretzels did a twist, The Swiss cheese yodeled when the chocolates kissed.

ALM

The tuna fish were singing tunes, over by the sink,
When the garlic joined in, they yelled, "YOU STINK!"

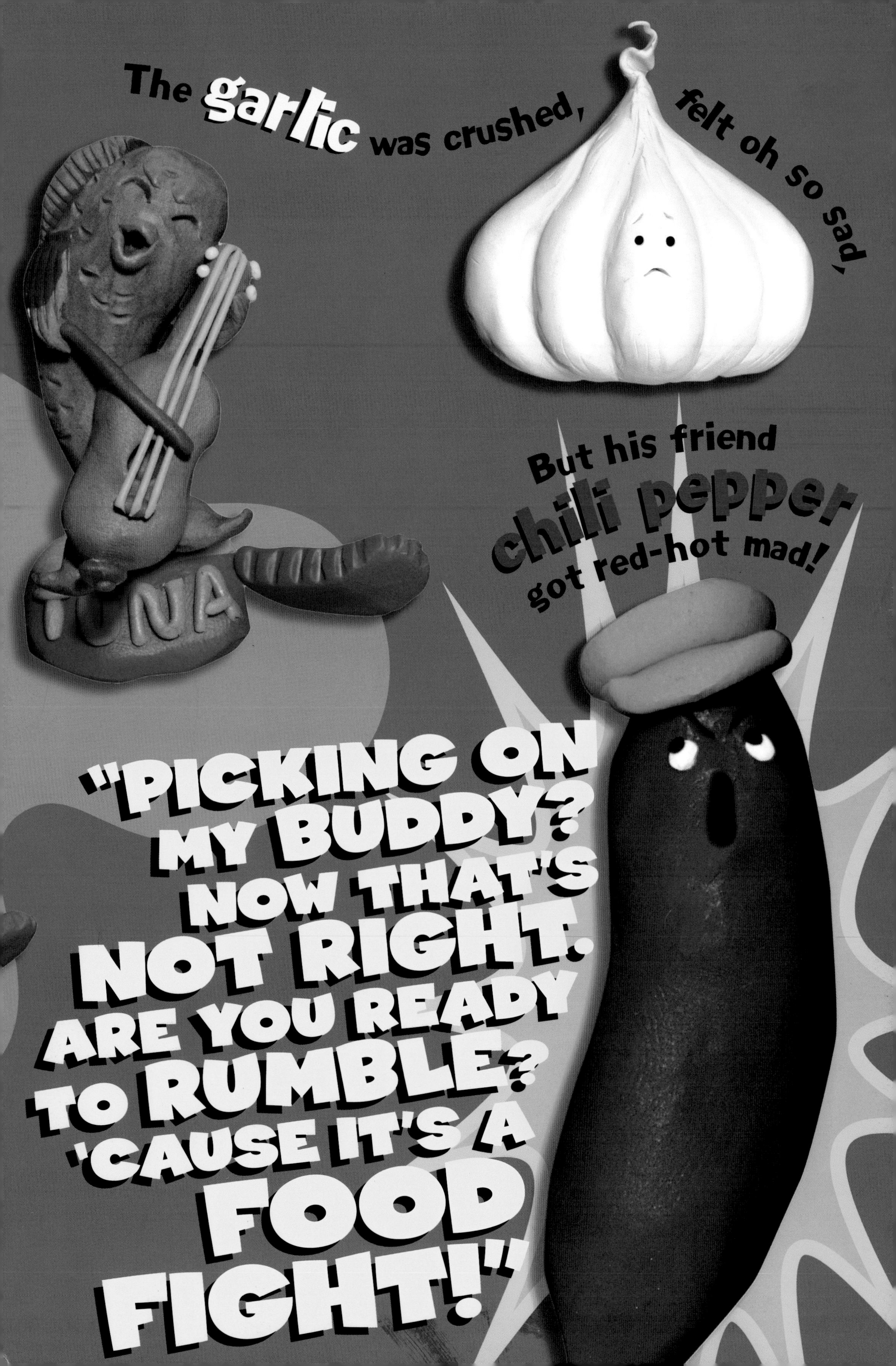

The **garlic** was crushed, felt oh so sad,

But his friend **chili pepper** got red-hot mad!

"PICKING ON MY BUDDY? NOW THAT'S NOT RIGHT. ARE YOU READY TO RUMBLE? 'CAUSE IT'S A FOOD FIGHT!"

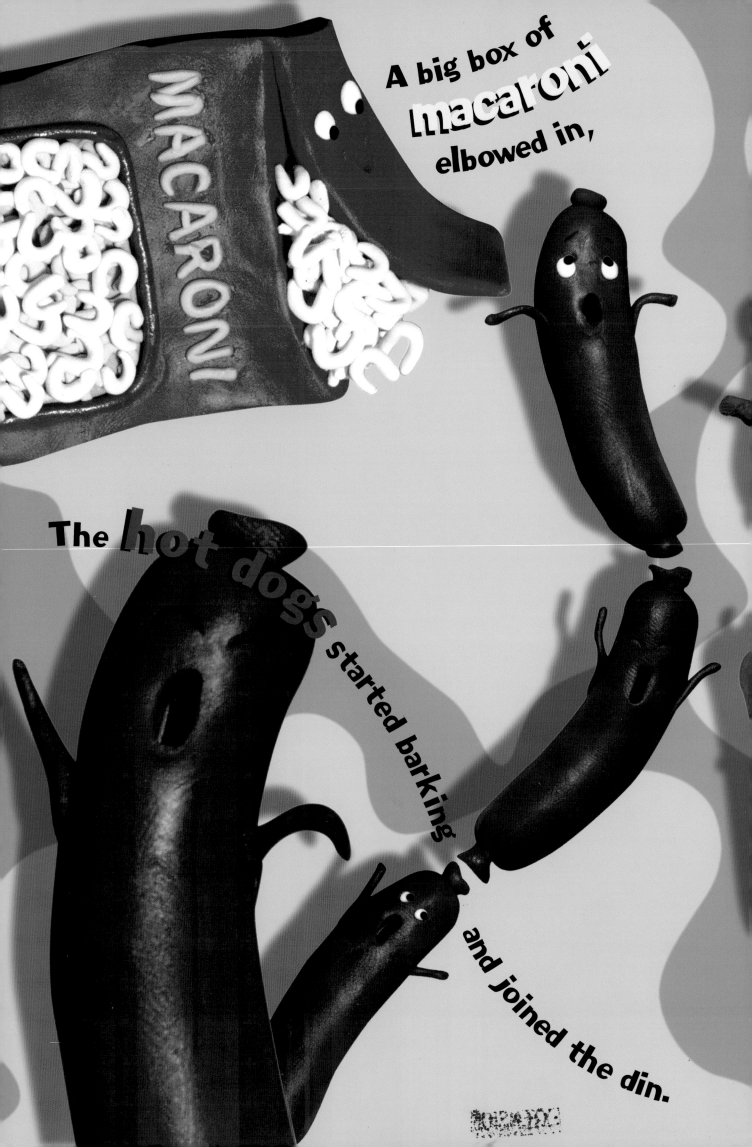

The chunky peanut butter jumped into the jam,

"YOU'RE CHICKEN!"

yelled the noodles to some soup in a can.

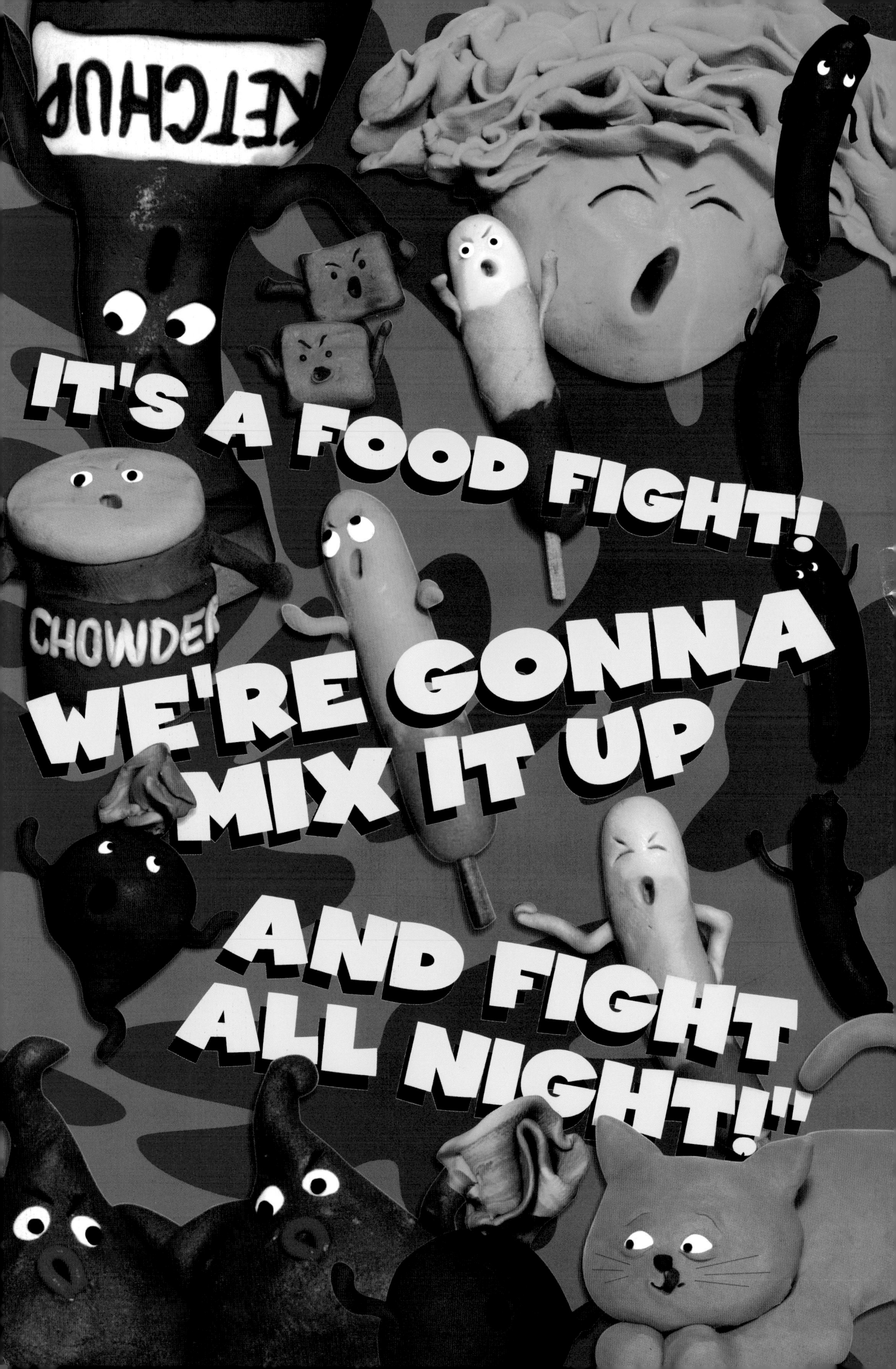

IT'S A FOOD FIGHT!

WE'RE GONNA MIX IT UP

AND FIGHT ALL NIGHT!"

And sure enough, from the vegetable drawer,
Ten Idaho potatoes rolled out on the floor.

They eyed the mess and then they scowled, "CLEAN IT UP NOW," the potatoes growled.

"PUT EVERYTHING AWAY AND DO IT FAST, OR COME TOMORROW MORNING, YOU'LL ALL BE TRASHED!"

The fight turned into
a clean-up race,
All the eggs scrambled
to get back in place.

The chowder
clammed up,

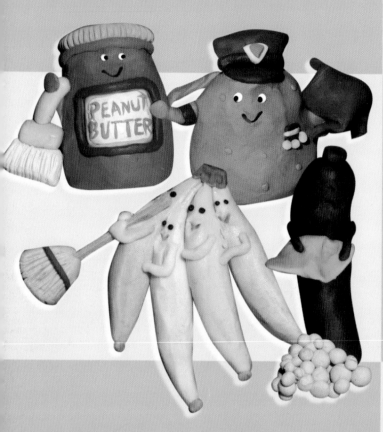

the bananas
peeled out,

The
Hamburger
Helper
scurried about.

The lights went out,
the broom swept away,

And everything was ready
for a brand new day.